Free

Patti Pelican and The Gulf Oil Spill

Copyright © 2011 by Lynda Wurster Deniger

Library of Congress Control Number: 2010918459

Lynda Wurster Deniger-
Patti Pelican and The Gulf Oil Spill

ISBN-13:   978-0-9831744-0-0

Other books by this author: SALTY SEAS & HIS HEROIC FRIENDS

For more information and to order: www.SaltySeasAndFriends.com

Published by: HIS PUBLISHING COMPANY
                   P.O. Box 147
                   Abita Springs, LA 70420
                   (985) 630-9867 (to schedule school performances)

Proudly Printed in the U.S.A. at
JOSTENS, Topeka, KS 66609

First printing March 2011

Publisher's Cataloging-in-Publication

    1.Deepwater explosion and oil spill 2010. 2. Oil spills, Mexico, Gulf of. 3. Louisiana–Social life and customs
    – Juvenile literature. 4. Environment and children. 5. Friendship. 6. Teamwork.

Illustrations: Paulette Ferguson
Book and Cover Layout: Caroline Blochlinger (www.cbAdvertising.com)

Thanks to Donnie Sanders for sharing his God-given talents with the "Salty Seas Series".

Patti Pelican
and
The Gulf Oil Spill

by Lynda Wurster Deniger

with Illustrations by Paulette Ferguson

Dedicated to the children whose hearts were touched by this terrible man-made tragedy. May God help us do a better job of caring for the marvelous world He created.

(Psalm 104)

Lynda Wurster Deniger's overwhelming success with **Salty Seas & His Heroic Friends** makes her the perfect storyteller to portray the heartbreaking events of the Gulf oil spill in an educational and uplifting style for children worldwide. She is a big hit with students of all ages during her school presentations. Call her to schedule one in your school.

Award-winning artist Paulette Vinyard Ferguson does it again with her exquisite true-to-life illustrations in **Patti Pelican and the Gulf Oil Spill**. Despite the serious nature of this disaster, Ferguson's appealing, child-friendly images soften the tragedy of the event and make it enjoyable for young children with the turn of each page.

Preface

About 40 miles off the coast of Louisiana on April 20, 2010, the Deepwater Horizon oil rig exploded into flames. The resulting oil spill lasted more than 100 days and would turn out to be the worst environmental disaster in United States history. By the time the leaking well, 5,000 feet below the water's surface, was capped in mid-July, close to 206 million gallons of crude oil had been released into the Gulf of Mexico.

The world was soon horrified by the photos of oil-soaked brown pelicans. The brown pelican, Louisiana's state bird depicted on its flag, its license plates and its state seal, had just been removed from the endangered species list. After 35 years of near extinction, the brown pelican's existence was threatened once again.

The International Bird Rescue Research Center, Tri-state Rescue Research, Louisiana's Department of Wildlife and Fisheries, and the U.S. Fish and Wildlife Service were all in a race to save as much of the wildlife as possible. Thanks to their unified efforts the lives of many of our precious birds and animals were spared.

Patti Pelican and Sammy Seagull of the "Salty Seas Series" share their experience in **Patti Pelican and The Gulf Oil Spill**. Patti, Sammy and I dedicate this story to these heroes of the environment.

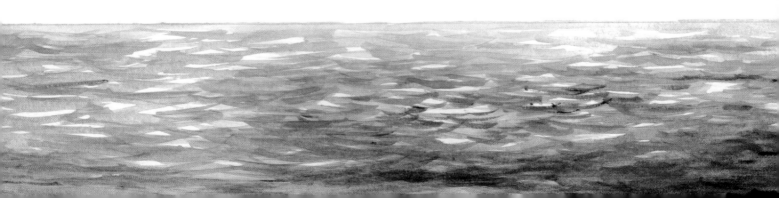

Shrimp season opens soon and excitement fills the bright, spring morning in Grand Isle, Louisiana.

Captain Charley finished rigging up the mended nets on Salty Seas.

"This year's going to be *our* year, Salty. We'll catch more shrimp than we did last year," Captain Charley said.

The radio announcer's booming voice interrupted the stillness. "There was a terrible explosion and fire on the Deepwater Horizon oil rig in the Gulf of Mexico last night. The well is still burning out of control."

"Did you hear that?" Captain Charley asked.

Patti Pelican plopped on her usual perch at Salty's steering wheel. "Hear what?" she questioned.

Flapping his wings and skidding onto the deck, Sammy Seagull yelled, "What? What? What happened? I missed that!"

"You're always missing something," Patti said.

Dottie Dolphin swam closer to hear the news that would change their lives for a long time to come.

In the days that followed, oil from the leaking well came closer and closer to Louisiana's fragile marshes. Fishing waters east of the Mississippi River were closed.

Unable to go fishing or shrimping, Salty and his shrimp boat friends volunteered to skim oil. They put out floating rolls of material called boom in an effort to capture the oil before it reached the shore.

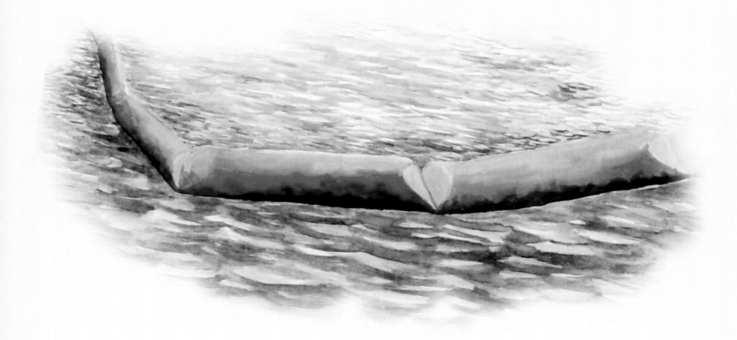

"I think I better swim far up into the bayou until the oil is gone," said Dottie.

"Maybe that's a wise decision" agreed Captain Charley. He was worried about the safety of Patti and Sammy, too.

While Salty and Captain Charley searched for oil, Patti and Sammy searched for food. Each time they dove into the oily water to grab a fish, the thick, brown tarry stuff coated their feathers until they could no longer move.

That afternoon when Patti and Sammy didn't show up at the dock to greet them, Captain Charley said, "Something must be wrong, Salty. We need to find Patti and Sammy right away."

He and Salty rode along the shoreline until they spotted them on the large pelican nesting grounds of Queen Bess Island.

Captain Charley jumped off the boat and into the shallow water. He scooped up the flying companions in a large fishing net, then radioed wildlife agents that he was bringing in two very oil-soaked birds.

"What will become of Patti and Sammy?" Salty asked when his friends were placed into large pet carriers and loaded onto an air-conditioned truck.

"I think we found them in time, Salty. They'll be in good hands and I'll stop by to check on them," said Captain Charley.

Once Patti and Sammy arrived at the rescue center, they were examined by a veterinarian. Identification bands were placed on their legs.

After a few days of rest, IV fluids, and food, Patti and Sammy were brought into the large washing area.

"What's up with those big silver tubs?" Patti asked.

"Uh, I don't know," replied Sammy.

Just then a lady with long rubber gloves placed Patti in one of those tubs and poured soapy water all over her, from head to claw.

A squawking Sammy was doused with warm, soapy water, too, followed by a powerful water rinse.

"Hey, watch it, Bub! You're gettin' water in my eyes," Sammy yelled.

"Yuck, this soap tastes terrible!" Patti said as they wiped her mouth out with a soapy rag.

"Keep your mouth shut, Silly!" Sammy screamed from across the room.

Moments later, a kind-looking man named Dr. Jay picked Patti up and gave her a gentle hug.

"Awwww. Can't you feel the love, Sammy? They're only trying to help."

The soaped, rinsed and dried Patti was transferred to a cage with other cleaned pelicans. "Hey, Guys. That sure was rough! I wonder what's next?"

"I need lots of rest and quiet," replied one of Patti's crate-mates.

Patti wondered how things could be quiet with Sammy making such a racket.

"Whew! Enough of that soap and water stuff. When do we eat?" Sammy questioned.

Sammy's spirits perked up when he spied the bucket of fresh fish. "Hey, Dude. Look at all that fish and I didn't even have to work for it!"

"See, I told you this place wasn't so bad," Patti said.

Soon Patti and Sammy were moved to outside cages where they bathed in fresh water pools, ate and exercised.

Patti and her new friends spent most of the day combing their feathers with their beaks so they would be waterproofed again.

Patti got news about her many relatives who were rescued and flown to Florida, Texas and Georgia to be released. A few injured white pelicans who had lost a wing had been sent to zoos all around America.

It wasn't long before Sammy was back to complaining. "When are we going home? I miss Captain Charley. I miss Salty. I miss Dottie."

"I do, too, Sammy. But we must wait until everyone here thinks it's safe for us to go home. I don't want to get back in all that oil."

A few days later Patti and Sammy were loaded back onto an air-conditioned truck. They rode several hours to the western side of Louisiana, which had not been affected by the oil spill.

Much to their surprise, Captain Charley and Salty were waiting at the dock to take them to Rabbit Island. They could hardly contain their joy of being together again.

Once the pet carrier door was opened, Patti and Sammy flew off side by side and landed on the crowded island where brown pelicans, laughing gulls, roseate spoonbills and other birds were nesting.

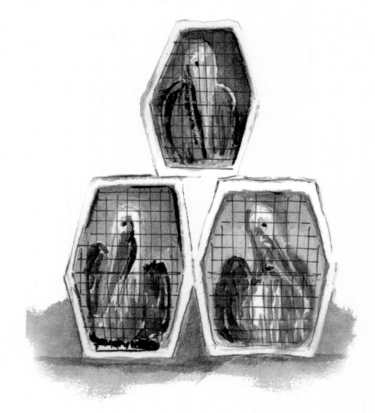

"Hey, Patti, this place looks alright. We can talk about plans to go home after we eat," said Sammy.

"Most of the oil is cleaned up and life is getting back to normal," said Captain Charley. "Why don't you two hang around here a while longer. We'll see you when you get home."

"Yeah, fish sounds good," Patti said.

"Going home sounds even better!" Patti and Sammy said in unison.

Epilogue

Children around the world were deeply touched by the plight of Louisiana's wildlife. Here are a few ways that children along the Golf coast reached out to help.

One New Orleans child offered to sell his toys to help the pelicans. His mom suggested they sell lemonade instead. His "Pelican Aid Lemonade" stand collected over $500 before he went to take a nap.

A Baton Rouge boy designed t-shirts and sold them to friends and neighbors. His $5,000 donation helped with the rescue of wildlife at the Audubon Institute.

Holding tin cans and signs saying "Pennies for Pelicans" and "Dimes for Dolphins", young girls from Houma purchased bandanas to cool the necks of wildlife agents in the field.

Maybe you can think of ways you could help save our wildlife. If you like to bake, maybe you could have a neighborhood bake sale. Maybe you could do extra chores around the house to earn money to donate to rescue groups.

Maybe the work you've seen the animal rescuers do in this book has inspired you to become a wildlife rehabilitator, a veterinarian or a biologist. Or you just might be the scientist who invents a new energy source that can help us all become less dependent on oil. We must find alternative ways to fuel the things we use, because as long as we use oil, there is always the risk of spilling it and polluting our environment.

You can make a difference in our world today, simply by saving one bird at a time. How? By helping the organizations that rescue them. If we work together, we can find ways to protect our world and its wildlife.

Patti and Sammy's story reveals a hopeful future for the more than 1,200 birds that were rescued, rehabilitated and released back into the wild.

Tri-state Bird Rescue Research Inc. and the International Bird Rescue Research Center (IBRRC) led the rescue efforts in response to the Gulf oil spill.

Since 1971, IBRRC has been dedicated to saving oiled, injured and sick aquatic birds worldwide, from Alaska to South Africa, Latin America and the Gulf. For more information about their ongoing hard work, visit their website at www.ibrrc.org.

A portion of sales from this book is being donated to IBRRC to help them respond quickly to disasters, wherever they might occur. You can make a contribution online or by mail to:

The International Bird Rescue Research Center
4369 Cordelia Rd.
Fairfield, CA 94534

With special thanks to Dr. Jay Holcomb, Director of IBRRC, for his expert guidance and consultation on this book.

Rub A Dub...Two Birds in a Tub

by Donnie Sanders & Lynda Deniger ©2011

Patti Pelican and Sammy Seagull
Got into an oil spill out in the Gulf
They could not fly, with their feathers soaked
With nowhere to go, they could barely float.

They were sinkin' in-to the oily goo
They tried to swim but they had no luck
Well, who did this? Where is the fool?
What's that I smell? Dead fish! Oh, Yuck!

CHORUS:

Oh, No! What shall we do?
Boo Hoo, looks like we're through
Boo Hoo, we're sinkin' in-to
This miry muck and this oily goo.

Toot! Toot! What's that I hear?
Toot! Toot! I think it's near
Toot! Toot! A pushin' through
Captain Charley's come to our rescue.

Rub a Dub, two birds in a tub,
Scrub, scrub, scrub,
We're scrubbin' them up.
We're gettin' rid of the miry muck
All of this goo and all of this yuck!

CHORUS:

Oh, No! What shall we do?
Boo Hoo, looks like we're through
Boo Hoo, we're sinkin in-to
This miry muck and this oily goo.

Toot! Toot! What's that I hear?
Toot! Toot! I think he's near.
Toot! Toot! Salty pushin' through,
Salty Seas come to our rescue.
Salty Seas come to our rescue.